'Six!' yelled Jess, as she ran past Tim and crashed into the shrubs. Thud! Her leg began to throb. She shifted the branches with her bat to get the ball.

'A nest!' yelled Jess. 'A nest with eggs in it!'
'Shush!' said Tim. 'You thrashed the branches with the bat and the mum dashed off. Hands off the nest, Jess, or she'll not come back. Let's get Dad.'

'It's a song thrush nest,' said Dad, 'a cup-nest of grass, twigs and mud. I think the mum will come back. Let's just sit, shall we?'

With a soft thud of wings, the song thrush dropped onto the path. She was plump with long, thin legs. She held a small shell.

Dad said, 'She will grip the lip of the shell and thump it on the path. It will smash and then she'll grab the snail and gulp it up.'

The song thrush thrust up her wings, swished up into the shrub and landed on the nest.

A month passed. It was the end of Spring.

'Dad!' Jess and Tim yelled. 'It fell from the nest! The nest is still there, but the mum is not in it.'

A small song thrush sat on the path. 'Hmm,' said Dad. 'I don't think it fell but it can't fly yet. Its mum must want it to begin to fly. There is a risk that a cat or a fox will get it.'

Jess sat still on the step. The song thrush's mum came back.
She fed it a slug. She helped it thrust its wings up, but it did
not fly. It fell.

Just then, a cat ran onto the path. Swish! Off dashed the song thrush's mum.

Jess ran and got her drum. Thump! Thump! Thump! The cat
ran off.

Tim sat still on the step. The song thrush's mum came back. She fed it a moth. She helped it hop and jump and thrust its wings up, but it still did not fly.

A fox crept across the long grass. Swish! Off went the song
thrush's mum.

Tim tossed balls at the fox. The fox came up the path. Tim's sixth ball hit the fox. Thump! The fox ran off.

Tim and Jess sat still on the step. It was dusk. The song thrush's mum came back. She helped it push off with its legs as it thrust its wings up. Lift off at last!

Tim and Jess were thrilled. Dad said, 'I think you kids did well.'
'Thanks, Dad,' grinned Tim and Jess.